HORIZONS

HORIZONS

SELECTED POEMS 1969-1998

STANLEY GREAVES

PEEPAL TREE

First published in Great Britain in 2002
Peepal Tree Press Ltd
17 King's Avenue
Leeds LS6 1QS

ISBN 1-900715-57-0

CONTENTS

THE CARTER POEMS

KIN

MEDITATIONS

METAPHYSICS

PEBBLES

HEARTLAND

MORTALITY

HARD YEARS

LAND OF GREEN

Dedicated to Martin Carter (in particular)
and the "Sunday Salon" c. 1978 – 82
Bill Carr, Mike Aarons, and Raymond Mandal.

THE CARTER POEMS

"Tree-tall friend of
a thousand conversations"

#1 POETRY

In the time of revised spells
when the language of poetry
is no more the tool of fools,
granite flowers will bloom
on the mountains, where
determined rivers flow
in furrows clawed by jaguars.

1978.

2# TO A POET M.C.

And the horses
And the drums,
the night does not still
dogs practising to howl.
With leaves stuck to feet
the condemned commit miseries
which even lilies in their hearts
cannot devotedly conceal.

The absence of truth
hoods the eagle's eyes,
angels cannot be heard,
only the warden of words
stringing poems,
as the precipitous wren
its galaxy of songs.

1979.

#3   FOREWORD

Two lines formed with words
spoken by Martin Carter, begin this poem.

"Your name is walking about
in a country of sprinting men."
The wordless meat of memory
is a vision mystery of encompassing
and the anxiety of a remembered curse.
Let the chessmen play!
The plural toe pads my solace,
and yet all around
unconscious slavering
nettles the skin into forgetting
the constituent assembly of humanity.

1981.

4#   FAREWELL

Tree-tall friend
of a thousand conversations,
peace between us
has always transcended
known boundaries of arrogance,
seeking, with feeling born
in envelopes of concern,
that numinous domain
of cautious mysteries,
welcoming as the earth is
for every floating seed
on stairs of air and rain.

I remember a fellowship,
walking between adamant trees
with singing bottles
from indescribable points.
No longer now can I witness
your quotidian presence
like precarious trees
beside a forwarding river.
Memories like sharp shadows
create yet sharper image
from the blunt turmoil
of dumb separation.

1987.

5#   TO MARTIN

Sadness and joy
a paradox of feeling,
of participating in
that special function,
the condition of friend.

1993.

6# LAST SUPPER

Lone so far,
each word dropping
like corn
from elevated cob.
what is a poem,
but the main course
of some fabulous feast.
Poet – head of table,
visitors, guests
sampling each line
as succulent slice.
Applause becomes sauce,
each shining verse
accepted, digested,
becomes the centre
of yet another story
of yet another poem,
elsewhere.

1995.

7# TIME I

Wizened fruit
crumpled can
underfoot the poet,
ubiquitous witnesses
to the collapse of time.
In magical instance,
that dot in sky or sea

conversant with
his mote-in-eye,
becomes phantom craft
or painful poem.

Can poets claim sovereignty
within the house of time.

1996.

8#   THE POET'S GATE

I boxed the face of the dog
with a book of poems.
It was more difficult
to deal with the gate
as with the poet's words,
dense intractable meanings
locked fast like kernels
in shells of hardest Brazil.
Between webs of words spoken
and rails of words written,
I sensed an enigmatic land
peopled by metric meteors.

Seated by his indulgent window,
I fitted his words between
leaves of listening balsam
like some fastidious carpenter,
wondering why today's relevance

19

is tomorrow's redundancy,
and why that dog is
still standing
at the gate.

1996.

9#   THE HERO

The hero steps
from his obvious shadow
into realms of the shadow.
The profoundest path
is made easy, like
walking on whispering shells.
What the foot knows
the mind now hears.
There is no horizon of limit,
fruits can fall upwards,
fingers challenge eyes
in the test of loving skin.

The stepping hero
loiters in metric maze
and disputes now
what he knew then.

He would not be hero,
but first stepping poet
of certified intent.

1996.

10# MARTIN

And what do you think
of a voice that oft-times speaks
in lines of sheer poetry.
It seems a halting here,
a darting there, fish
or bird of relentless poignancy.
The wonderment of that word
plucked like honey/kernel
of intransigent flower/nut.
That flash and falling –
bright sudden meaning.
What do you think of
voices that now speak
in lines of sheer poetry.

1997.

11# THERE IS A POEM HERE

There is a poem here,
lines of layered meanings, and
surprises like twisted commas.
Object and dream become words,
words flex to symbols.
Rhythm, a net to trap souls
while symbols, just so, fly
in portentous conjunctions.
Dread accompanies meaning
and red silence follows
impatient marks on paper.

Eyeless in the night
ambition awaits the poet,
the poet, that sometime meaning
rising with delayed dawn.
There is a poem here.

1997.

12# THE LAST WALK

I write to you, I write to you
and so a plangent tale is born,
like old Cuffy, Atta, Akkara
and the fateful siege of Dageraad,
as Guyaná now, enshrouded in
the curse of ballots of deceit.
In the very streets you walked
smoke and bullets seek victims
awaiting the elusive count, the way
young lovers and salient memories
haunt the grey adamant wall
that created a long haunted coast.

Oh parlous day! Oh parlous day!
The votive streets you often danced
stand strangely still and enchanted
like Chinese landscapes you loved.
In bye-ways, shadows absent themselves
as your being, now bereft of words,
is drawn by horses of wondrous form
worshipped in your cosmic visions.
The litany of priest and family, and
unfamiliar constraints of church,

even hymns must have seemed strange,
but not the songs of grace you loved –
"Where have all the flowers gone!"
of proclaimed and private triumph,
your family Wylde and far Ireland.

The gods of Parnassus, name place
like some ruined Guyana plantation,
must have in deliberation drawn
the ironic circle of chanting citizens
hurling political names in fury along
your last walk to a defined space,
fury often limned in adamant lines
living in your trenchant poems
refuting seasons of pernicious politics.

Sentinels of trees, salute of proud guns
greet you – "the poems man", borne
in a flag-draped boat of purple wood
riding a tide of true lucid poems
on that journey eternally defined by
welcoming Osiris in green and black
and Isis attending in robes of white
celebrating the truth of life and death –
a demanding mantle you proudly wore.
I write to you, I write to you, finally
and so a plangent tale is born.

1999.

KIN

"Small hands that delight in the smoothness of pebbles"

S. GREAVES '99

13#   FAMILY

My mother
my sister
my wife
all soft-bellied
like the ocean.
My father
my brother
and I
all furious at life,
like winds over waves.

1962.

14#   ORIGINS

The origins are obscure,
and lineage doubtful.
All I have to reckon by
is the colour of my mother's skin
and the colour of my father's eye.

1976.

15#   POWER   *(to Ivan Greaves)*

Come drink my brother
but do not sing.
Let petals fall in grace
and prayer rise over
the benediction of flowers.
In the want of time
a whole civilization
will erupt in song.

Praises my brother
are best not heard.
Real power resides
in the map of a hand
and not in ambience.
The caprice of ambition
constructs ironical events,
for shouted statutes
do not apply to stars.

1981.

16#   TASHIE

Two faces in the heart of a child
and the heavy parting of eyes,
body blood shapes its being
along departing shadows
and memories of undeclared love.

1983.

17#   UNCLE JOHN.

Through the window
by your bed,
I see stunted sorrel plants
fight the tight yellow earth.
I listen out of time
as your child-voice,
grown out of manhood,
reaches some trite memory
taut as a kite-string.

It was here
in your somnolent room
I learnt companionship
is many things.
The commonplace
has a point.

1984.

18#   BLACK SUN *(to Ivan Greaves)*

Black sun
complex horizons.
What is it
we cannot reach
yet touched
we shudder.

1988.

19#   DE PROFUNDIS II   *(to Mum, Priscilla).*

I did not cry
when my Father died,
instead a picture was painted.

I did not cry
when my mother died,
but paid visit
to a silent sea.

Death is as expected
as it is unexpected,
and that holy surprise
cannot really be shared.

But as I left the sea,
I was suddenly reminded
that the salt of my tears
and that of the waves
was the same.

1995.

20#   TO JOHN AND PRISCILLA G

Above the horizon
the dive of every bird
questions the existence
of daily air,
as every sealed tomb
the story of life.

Hope of heaven,
onetime familiar wish
takes on strange meanings,
as the sight of a piece
of twisted paper releases
promises past and present.

1995.

21# TO FAKHIA *(a welcome)*

A bell will ring
with the sound of a flower.
Miriam at crossroads
will laugh in an ancient way.

Love can be a cryptic force,
continents and cultures
mere intrusive toys,
or love becomes exquisite fruit
of passion and commitment.
A bell will ring
with the sound of a flower.

1996.

22#   ISABELLA.

Spend a little time with me
and I will sing you a song
of quiet simple joys.
Strange the world
to new still eyes and
meaningless sounds to ears.
But stranger still
is the music of rain
and small birds bathing,
toads mimicking rocks,
and roads with no end.
Small hands will delight
in the smoothness of pebbles
and tongue to eager spoon.
But of all such things
most enduring will be,
voices near and far
that will always say —
We love the wonder of you.

1999.

MEDITATIONS

"The square in the circle
is a dream in a dream"

S. GREAVES '99

23# PRAYER

Devil is behind God's back
as God is behind the Devil's.
If one forgets you
the other will not.

Man's need to pray
seeks any willing mystery,
be it tide at rest
the mountain's face,
or web of time and space.

1976.

24# YEAR OF CHILD AND FLOWER

Yesterday today and
tomorrow's flower
born without adjectives,
What hero can match
the exactitude of a bud.

Pink glimpse of the world,
pristine thoughts in
dappled nectarine cadence,
Oh perfumed child!
Oh spirited flower!

1979.

25# HOMAGE TO A BERBICIAN CHILD

Innocent abroad,
and sacred tree
whose fruit became
the death apple.
Blind wishes,
by some flaw of logic,
created fatal strokes
upon that child
tied to a tree.
What must the leaves say
in the primal void
of that moment,
when man recreates
the legend of hate.

1979.

26# FISHENING

Trenched internal auditors,
anglers of unresolved helixes
whose immutable designs
bait the infinities
of crossed horizons.
The concision of a line
is an intolerable burden
focussed in an eye.

When thoughts fish-rise
to challenging fingers
action is paramount.
Sweet rain and skin.

1980.

27# QUESTION.

With an egg on my shoulder
I question the sea,
not knowing the power
protecting this laughing child
from eves-dropping souls,
in the shadow of that gate.

Silence contemplates
a small falling leaf,
no sound challenges
this intrusive laughter
born of an ancient will.

1986.

28#   GUESTS

In the shadow of a black ant
my spirit stood darkly,
although the sun watched
in benign contradiction.
We do not choose moments
when thoughts rise like
a blanket of moss and bubbles
from boundaries of mud,
but yet must we accommodate
those unwelcome guests,
as we do those far flung lights
of prophetic patterns
that invade the bowl of night.

1987.

29#   SILENCES   I

Go softly into the stranger night,
while the tapestry of collective wish
living in an apprehension of morning
rests in the uneasy peace of footfalls
passing small rooms called home.

The face across my table whispers.
The dark window calls.
Each perception like tendrils
claws the air to extend root-self

in daunting ever-changing prospect
of exploring that space
and strange dimensions waiting.

1987.

30#   SILENCES II

Darkness has no dimension
so is the volume of a dream.
Morning brings a luminous measure
to my room of a still bed
and memories of stray moments.
Two punctured petals of rose
rest between lines of the floor
like voices and informed music,
inviting the cold bare floor
to welcome walking steps
measuring a reluctant day.

1987.

31#   IT AND NOT IT

This quiet time,
this singular hour
conjuring voices I wish
would speak to others,
welcoming that blackness
that is not the absence
of light, but that residence
of reflex purpose.
It and not it.

1991.

32#   NAVIDAD

Love your sister?
I am sure
you have heard,
or imagined,
pointless whispers
of anxious friends.
The stories told of
accepted pregnancy
coming from nowhere,
or so it seemed.
Moment of revelation
impacted like
semen on seed.
The world changed
in a second.
Aunt – not mother.

1995.

33#   PASSING THOUGHT

The night seems too long,
is there no end to this vale
of trees and dreams?
Each leaf has edge and point
and drifts to dimensions.
Where is that edge and point
of dedicated consciousness,
in whose ledger of opacity
will an infallible logic appear?
To be confounded is real hell.
The spirit in boots of lead.

1966.

34#   HATE STONE

And why should I not
speak of the dead,
if in dying they clutch hate
to their chest
like a stone.

In living, hate lives,
in dying so should it,
but not to endure eternity
while those hated live.

The emblazoned leaf of love
is errant adversary

to the fire ink of hate.
After every lightning stroke,
a forest of compassion
always grows.

1997.

35#   ESSAY

Love loves loving
in the essay of life.
For the act of loving
what will be or whence
criteria of taste –
whose fingers to unravel
skeins of feeling.
An essay on life is
the essay of love,
something about doing
and not about writing.
Criteria comes from heart
not from crabbed words.
Differences between landscape
and any printed page –
between perception and process
define one another
as bat and fruit in air.
So love loves loving
and hate absorbed.
The essay of life lived.

1998.

METAPHYSICS

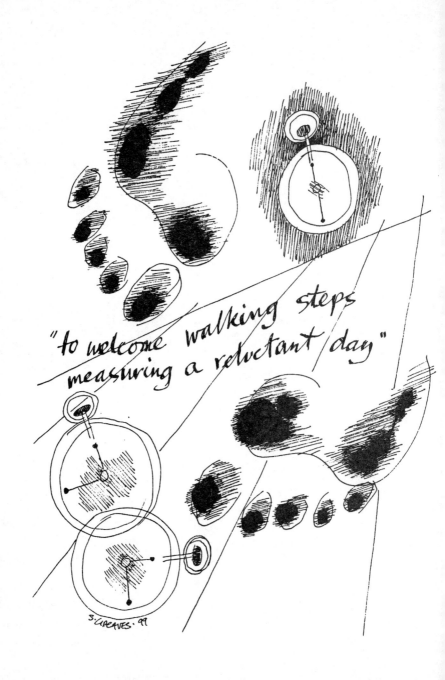

"to welcome walking steps
measuring a reluctant day"

S. GREAVES. 99

36#   CATEGORIES

Dog dung
cat shit
cow dung
bull shit
donkey dung
fowl shit
bat dung
monkey shit
goat rolls
fly specks,
and for humans…
and for humans?
EXCREMENT.

1973.

37#   PYTHAGORUS' DREAM

The square in the circle
is a dream in a dream.
Reality lies at a point,
point at centre.

Who knows what lies
at the centre of a dream
within a dream.

1975.

38#   WAITING SONG

In life's static moments
sing your waiting song.
Although rapacity is a badge
flaunted in mimic brotherhood
of the plural polyp,
strict measures of feeling
hymn inflected grace
in the instant of affirmation
daunting stone avarice.

To merely notice
is not to recognise
the integrity of sand.

1981.

39# DERELICTION

From this chrysalis
dreams take stuttered flight.
Dereliction as form
attracts events
of certified colour,
– like plaintive rags
and shattered leaves.

1984.

40#   HORIZON

Until now
one horizon was enough.
Until now,
the sky was a secret place
to fishes who finally understood
that clouds have horizons,

1984.

41#   LIVING

Sweet knife, trusting flower,
colour is not the issue
nor shaping shadow-leaf
wordless yet close, as
shapeless heartbeats.

Living is discovering
the unflinching correspondence
of dialogue as paradox,
between seeing and knowing
when that strident horizon
describes now,
both knife and flower.

1989.

More water
more farms
more food
more children
more houses
more garbage
more industries
less resources
more pollution
less forests
more deserts
less water
less farms
less food
less children,
more becomes less,
less becomes more,
of what?

End of story.

1991.

43# CATBOX

A box with holes,
home for a cat.

Real dark,
with a real hole
black,
is beyond
cat, box, or home.

1994.

44# NEW ALGEBRA

This closing of functions,
this strange algebra.
If A means breath
and B, sleep,
X and Y propose
equations of final order.
Language once free
in eye and tongue, now
declaims N the constant.
New love, new everything,
closing ancient equations
to set the new algebra.

1995.

45#   CONNECTION

This palpable box
this consciousness
within consciousness,
point within a point
paradox place
of no dimensions.
Tangibility is not
one of the questions,
it is that interface,
that ineluctable plane
or unspeakable horizon,
flexing wondrously
like practising wings.
Flight, not air,
is one real connection
between bat and butterfly.
Flight , like consciousness
here, and here again,
and yet, like the butterfly
can we know the connection
between colour and flight?

1996.

A foot is no more
        a club
as knife
        a leaf.
And yet foot can strike
        as any club.
Extension of acts and meanings
make a thing other than itself.
Shaded chameleons
illustrate the axiom.
Joseph's coat intervenes –
        colour makes the man.
The question:
        Who owns colour?
        Colour owns whom?
The riddle:
        It is not the answer
        but rather the question
        that owns the questioner,
Or is it?

1996.

47#   RIDDLE   II

Major third to minor third,
minor to major,
an indulgent image
as we to our shadow.
Who or what questions which?
What else is constituent
to acknowledge parallel states
where simple finger meets
hypothetical point,
and slow eyes roam
indulgent planes bounded
by flagrant horizons.

It is but an enchanted riddle
as all true riddles are.
What can any answer be
in such exalted context but
a gesture of open palms
and fingers flung to the wind.

1997.

48#   HUBRIS

Bird and bat
play with air,
fruits belong to
anchored trees.
Man looks to sky

sees clouds go by
and dreams ever
about destiny.

So kites and rockets
symbolically born
play against planets.
Arrogance and imagination
provide crude strategies
for games against gods.

But they who walk
cannot really fly,
and struggle endlessly
in the provocative web
of impartial gravity.
Squares are not cubes.

1997.

49#   TEACHER

The challenge of teaching,
unceasing combat with
the mystery of things.
What really is…A
whence is the shape of…8.
To think the word EAT
relates to spoon and teeth.
Is it the teacher's task
to dilute innocence
in cultures of explanation,
or, secretly wish that

in a somewhere time,
innocence as fantastic bird
will take resolute flight
to refute cultures
that wear boots.

1997.

50# TIME II

There was a time
when there was no time,
and the legends began
of impossible beasts
and incredible heroes
whose graves we cannot find.
As we look through
clear air or empty rooms
one timeless question appears.
Is there a place, some
imperturbable windless place
where thoughts eventually go.
Are the sensations of time
part of the time of time,
some miracle of construction
like bone sinew feather, or
mysterious relation between
lung and spoken word.
What would it be if
I really knew time.

1998.

51#   RELATIONSHIP

What is stick to stone,
those lips to a cloud.
Not so easy as
foot – shoe – road,
calculated events
beneath leaf or sea,
or behind stark words
of any prescient poem.

It is the extension of spirit
seeking to know, if
existence precludes
knowledge of itself,
Whether the commonplace
will always confound –
like fruit and stem
or foot and shadow.

To witness connections
is to enter a serial place –
some fabulous box of
unruly revelations
never to be captured
like bird or poem.

1998.

52#   GRASS-BIRD

To see and know that
a grain of rice, feather
or discarded nail
are fellow mysteries
as hearing and counting
heartbeats — now and now.
Mysteries they say
are here to be solved,
but solutions become
perverse shrunken shoes.
Aesop made fables
and we learn to see —
as grass-birds find seeds,
the waiting mysteries
beneath companion feet.

1998.

53#   LAND OF QUESTIONS

Oh strange anniversary!
Oh convoluted passage!
Expectation becomes an old shoe
prepared to renew itself.
Questions fall from the sky, like
symbols demanding time to
reveal themselves — if ever so —
in a place where answers
in dance-turn become questions.

But we must wait — always wait
in yet another place where
swift questions give eager birth
to even more questions.

1998.

54#   BUDDHA II

Buddha sits accompanied
by a small silent clock
on a bed of faded petals,
and still he smiles
with the earned assurance
of one who looks over the horizon.

Why do we become vexed if
fruits fall before ripening
and marvel when some
clouds cruise backwards.

There was a time when
the bright petals were fresh
and the bald silent Buddha
was already smiling.

1998.

Words that aim to define
never fit like skin on fruits,
there is always some space
accommodating other meanings.
Definitions, as any skin, ages
but like the mythic dragon
new skin replaces old,
the question re-invents itself
and answers take the field
against weapons of definition.
Visions in the heat of revelation
create words of self description
then vanish under them,
like some ant-covered beast.
Definitions are the slaves of words,
words the slave of visions.
Thus the unwelcome martyr,
borne by intrusive visions,
suffers the fate of those
daring to defy definitions.

1998.

56# PARADOX

Like heady dark wine
paradox presents itself
as experience within/without
the perception of events.
It comes as wild errant dancer
in changing robes to confound
those thinking of open freedoms.
It comes to delight those welcoming
stones that skip on water,
colours that disappear at night
along with the howling of dogs.
At such sudden stopped moments
those ubiquitous gifts of paradox
reveal the magic of experiences
in ribbons of consequences
that make each day infinite.

1998.

PEBBLES

"Deliberate steps to the gates of choice
beware of falling fruit."

57#   COSMO

I am Cosmo.
In my fluting veins
blood flows hard –
red, black, white
blue and green.
I am a Cosmo.
Today I am from Africa
Europe or India,
and think of China!
And the next day…
and the next?
I am a Cosmo…mo…mo.
Whoeee…
that means…
And that means
I …am…Me.

1975.

58#   CHILDHOOD

I walked along the avenue
of my childhood, And as always
the wind blew my steps away.
In the shadow of gentle trees
I watch soft raindrops change
into small birds of delight.

How loud is the clamour
of unbidden memories
upon the fragility of friendships
long gone. Like haze
upon the unrelenting severity of
a dispassionate horizon.

Images of time past are stored
in the back of a lonely mirror,
like leaves of a forbidden book.
And it is not sadness,
only the strange weary joy
of accessible inevitability,
newfound companion
on that same avenue
of yet another childhood.

1982.

59#   COMPANIONSHIP

Rumcup of solitude, and
air itself willing to breathe.
The things paths do I cannot,
and exponential trace of
when, where, and what,
is my indenture-ship.

Companionship is not talk —
is the whole murmur

of faint memorial shadows
from the corners of dreams –
is the green and gold.

1982.

60#   WISH III

Why should I be witness
to these inhabited rags
drifting wherever the road goes.
Why should my humanity
live in lingering outrage
at their dread configuration.
Through these people as mirror
I see my out-of-tune self
stumbling between eye and foot.
A single anxiety becomes stone
thrown against imperturbable glass
crazing to amazing web –
the longitudes and latitudes of man
from damp beggar to rampant king.
A wish to disengage falters.
I am left with thoughts
that cannot make men fly.

1985.

61# JUDGEMENT

If you were a judge, I would
empty my cap before you
in the face of night,
of the name of things
I wish to have,
and hide what I love
from market-place eyes.

Having walked without,
I return to that little room
filled with the mystery of colour,
and the thread I found leading
to the birthplace of death.

1985.

62# MORNING-SONG

PREFACE:
*The opening line, parting words
from my Mother one morning,
caused this poem to be written.*

The morning is dry,
beetles have lost the race
against the rise of the sun.
On a bed of rumpled dreams
I encounter complexities between
things that come by night
and what the eyes see by day.

Knocks on my door,
conversations that go nowhere,
footfalls and two notes
of the singing frog
propound the question of
what to do with silences.

The morning is dry
and beetles have lost the race.

1986.

63# TANNEWERKE (*Princess of Ethiopia*)

Strange soft images
rise in the mind,
like opalescent buildings
of steel and glass
upon an ancient street.
Today's and tomorrow's room
face the same horizon
of duty replacing desire.

In some unbidden place
an Ethiop princess
in two-dimensional austerity,
watches from the wall of
womanhood's life of power,
and I, a little boy
of multiplication tables
and laughing shoes
play with dreams.

1987.

64#   SCHOOLDAYS

Every nun wears a ring
– Brides of God.
An astonishing act,
as if depictions of hell
came true with brush-marks
and artists cheering.

Rain is wetting windows,
but what about trees
witnessing the Bride of God
deprive little boys of sin.

For each nun, God and boy,
strings of colour
and separate balconies
link all realities as
another astonishing act.
But the sunset is yours,
the garden of guavas mine,
and God can have the rest.

1990.

65#   ENCOUNTER

What do I do.
– Just wait – she said,
   and let the thing
   happen.
I have been waiting
since,
and seen many things
happen –
but not that.

1994.

66#   CONTROL

The car
I control,
and brushes.
But what about
one grey hair
out front,
or tears,
or snail
on sunlit fence?

1994

67#   EFFORT

I am in no race, but
heartbeats speak otherwise
of spectral crowds,
small flags on grass,
and medals of false metal.

Effort is the thing,
repeatedly repeated
among things anchored
all around, whenever,
in that particular space,
the mythic mind of culture.

1996.

68#   CHOICES

Personal active, impartial passive,
what you do and what is done.
Deliberate step to gates of choice,
beware of falling fruit.

I made myself enter wedlock with art,
but within a conspiracy of events,
the equation reversed –
Art chose!

So like the pendulum we swing,
orphan to grandparent
giddy day to infinite night.
Personal active, impartial passive.

1997.

69#   OUT-HOUSE

In a box
I sit on this hole
in a senseless plank.
Through another
hole, crevice, crack,
I witness
the frolic of birds
and bright flies
in light and space.

The real wonder is me,
in singular connection
between roiling maggots,
the frolic of birds
and bright flies.

1997.

70#   DOLL AND FLOWER

*A synchronous event about a doll
involving two countries.*

Far far flower is red
like a distant doll robed
in proscriptive sunlight.
Intrinsic connection –
as remembered self
between rock and I standing
between far flower, distant doll –
is always that elusive fruit
shining upon itself.

Similar meanings elsewhere
like thoughts released
course between leaves
and make trees talk.
Listening becomes discovery
commodity or experience -
or song of my infallible strings
between far far doll
and distant red flower.

1999.

71#   EXILE

I may as well
retreat into realms
of an obscure aesthetic,
as share my findings with
a table with no legs.

So long have I laboured
on sunlit steps, or
in fixed cramped rooms
devoid of meaning.

Leaves from the tree of time
create memorable carpets
of condemnation or approval,
and I must continue yet
to live in such ambience,
noticed as but a raindrop
on the hot black road.

1997.

72#   FIRST DANCE

An invitation to the party came
all neat like an egg with a tie,
and you felt happy and steady
like that framed photo on the wall.
Trembling "what ifs" and "buts"
attack new dressed-up thoughts.
"What if she asks you to dance!"
square-up yourself like biscuits,
let "yes" fall as eager mangoes do.
Shoes will move easy as butterflies
toes won't know where they are.
"Of course you care", she's with you.
Move like the flag on a windy day,
savour the moment eternity long
when the song without end begins.

1997.

73#   TO MY BANKER

Respected Sir,

    With studied reference
to the letter of the 13th,
I had offered cubed hopes
on the bureaucratic altar
of golden expectancy.

    Your words like deliberate
rocks from a malignant sling
have wrecked my anchorage.
Now, like battered flotsam I lie
on oceans of indifferent sand,
deprived of my birthright to salt.

Respectfully yours,

1997.

74#   THE THIRD DOLL

This first fateful doll
dressed in warm eyes,
came in a simple box
and changed a life.
There were things
that fell into place
and things that did not.
I am ever reminded of
that doll who came

as unexpected prize.
Unexpected gift, not prize
was the next doll,
small and very bright –
construct of perception
time and fate perchance –
connection between
flower, shoe, star-fall
and any familiar location
like green hedge gray post.
Numbers are vital, I know,
and so curiously alarmed
await the third doll.

1998.

75#   GEOMETRY

I know the subtle terror
of past and future tangents
to my circle self.
The stark world of Euclid
and ancient marks on stone
I range – committed hunter
of meanings elusive as
wise deceptive animals
in open universal nights.

It is an impersonal world
where lines and angles
of unbidden thoughts
dance entrancing geometries.

But do I need to know
where is the home of meanings?

1998.

76# WISH IV

Is it your wish –
as strange as wishes go
that continually
I renew my presence
like the cat with bird-gifts.
Renewal and change
are not the same leaves
though of the same tree.
That wish for surprise
becoming eternal delight
makes us the child playing
with forbidden matches –
Will it flower to flame?

Change should change
our perception of pleasure,
yet we long to swim twice
in what seems the same river
though the ancient one said,
We cannot step twice,
however, in that place.
Do not look then for surprises
in wrapped occasional boxes,
look instead for other gifts
in my not-the-same eyes.

1998.

77#   REVERIE (*to Rimbaud*)

> *Engorgé du sang*
> *Engorgé de l'esprit.*

I heard a squeak and thought,
with familiar arrogance,
it was because of me.
The howls of everywhere-dogs
roam the same spaces
night-spirits in-dwell –
and the roaring in my ears.

> *Filled with blood*
> *Filled with spirit.*

How difficult to know others,
instead, I think of myself – easy,
but in time's geography
where is her spirit
this moment in voyage.
Such cryptic patterns as,
thought, dogs, spirit, night,
complex as silent diamond
traps any inquisitive vision.

> *Filled with blood*
> *Filled with spirit.*

At the end – the rooster's vigil –
timing must be right
in that burst or instant
for the sun must always rise.

Events briefly fleshed
by implied alchemy, present
memory as skipping residue.

> *Filled with blood*
> *Filled with spirit.*

1998.

78#   MEMORIES

I picked up a pin,
crumpled printed paper,
talked to the cat
and my subsequent self.
Casual moments, now
swallowed by time I
would think about, but
dress with flawless fantasy
memories that forgot to breathe.
And while tomorrow is new,
experience cannot be re-eaten,
nor hauled from the sky
like loud reluctant kite.
My shadow knows where
I have ever walked, and
can never walk again.

1998.

HEARTLAND

" never paints rainbows
for ants running my mind"

79#   LILY AND THE LEAF

Ahead lies the garden
where kisses make flowers grow
and whispers water them.
You be the lily and I, the leaf
to catch each jewel
falling from your eyes,
and in that hour
when the sun becomes
a glowing blue worm
cocooned by clouds
I shall string you
a necklace of gossamer.

1962.

80#   DREAM OF PHAROAH'S DAUGHTER

On a blanket of stars
collecting dimples,
I listen to your eyes
and hear smiles
as the clock throws
each long second away.

Three doves in a circle
move away far far,
in sympathy with waves
and sharp intervals
of secret crickets.

Dear sister of Egypt,
like the perfume
of temple flowers,
let songs fly
from your fingertips.

1979.

81#   LONGTIME

If lines in my hand
have become my face,
you have been a long time coming.
The ecstasy of clouds
never paints rainbows
for ants running my mind,
and I did not recognise your face
bringing birds, who
shelter under divine love.

Jaguar, stone-flower,
you have been a long time coming.
Each day is today
for tomorrow never comes
to steal my shadow
of exultant bouquets.

1980.

82#   LAMENT

Last night's passing star
is but a little death.
How easy to answer
the questions others ask
in unanswerable acts of mine.

In the stream of time
premature urgings become
the matter of cubed thoughts,
Like a boat in a sea of leaves,
a child skating in a window,
and the cryptic chemistry
of star-fire dreams.

1981.

83#   FRIENDS.

Fingertips and flowers
small feathers, sweet birds
and spaces between words.
The courtly dance of friends
is an iris of surprise,
soft-eared words and
a feeling native to self.

Around the festival table
of hearts flowers and music,
gossamer memories
of an ancient face provoke

the dynamics of reality –
change within change,
the challenging dream where
the moth flew brushing my lips,
like the startled fingers
of a breathless child
playing with newfound fear.

1981.

84#   DE PROFUNDIS I

Today,
I did not go
to the ocean.
Instead,
it came to me
somehow
through tears.
No sorrow,
no joy
nor else,
save that they came.

Boats and feelings
should have only sails
and a wish
elemental,
as flags and arrows.

1981.

85# WAITING SONG

In life's static moments
sing your waiting song.
Although rapacity is a badge
flaunted in mimic brotherhood
of the plural coral polyp,
strict measures of feeling
hymn inflected grace
in the instant of affirmation.
To merely notice
is not to recognise
the integrity of sand.

1981/97

86# ISSAFAYA

Flames of a new sun register
the birth of pink orchid
unfolding and glorious
in the fastness of the forest.

Fey sister, Faya flower,
so far way from home
whose corners and dust
were welcome friends.
Soft jaguars and bird-songs
become newfound friends.
The distance genes measure
lies between eyes.

1981.

87#   OREMA

Footfalls predict shadows,
as a finger anticipates
the direction of a vine
curling upon itself —
exploring linkages.

Grief, privately gentle, somewhere
contemplates the exodus of love,
wondering whether a moment
is anything but that which
confounds thought,
like the flash of a green sun
or the unnoticed annihilation
of spark to air.

1983.

88#   DAZUMA.

Was smoothness to ivory
the same my hand felt
over landscarped hip
of infallible tissue.

Wilderness and eyes
have a singular dedication
to inscrutable black.
Night offers a sigh
and the mad delight of shadows
and the shaping of starred rain.

1984.

89#   SHIRLEY STAR-APPLE

How I envied that skin
so magnificent in the sun,
like green and purple,
so textured, like the fuzz
of a bright star-apple leaf
to eye and hand.
Fruits are without artifice,
the presentation is
be sucked or cut.
Taste becomes experience
straight and transcendent
like fruits forever falling.
But you magnificent
in black, green and purple
were never sucked or cut
in tides of sun or moon.

1996.

90#   NOW

If I lost the letters
but kept the flowers,
what can they tell me.
Time may not heal
breaches in memory
carved by insistent images
of remembered hurt.
But, as the bird sings,

new days bring joy
fresh as flame flowers.
The meaning of life
is dimensions of now.

1997.

91# SLEEP AND WAKE

The night sighs dark,
weaving tenebrous fabrics
to shade my dreaming face.
A conspiracy of sensations
construct stark events of
grand absurdist meanings
during syllables of sleep.
And what about waking
when brittle bodies resemble
amalgams of strange constructs?
Have you really looked at
hip, ankle, a wrist, foot —
sometimes described beautiful
as a night of stars.

Each station of consciousness,
relevant monochrome sleep or
open-dawn day of scented hope,
paints inconsistent pictures —
a crab walking on blue plate.
The thing is to draw a line,
infallible horizon linking

consequences of day and night,
and to walk that same line
and damn any fear of falling.

1998.

92#   ANNIVERSARY

A present for you
on behalf of today.
This celebration is like
a one legged stool
that needs a sitter
in order to stand.
So must you be the sitter
and I the stool
to recognise this day –
any anniversary day
spent in stern wonder
of a single moment
of indescribable meeting.
Mutual eyes forever
make time timeless.

1999.

93#   MARENTHA

At parched earth's voice
give rain not pennies
to trees and fingered grasses.
Drought's coup d'etat
makes my scorched spirit
suffer in dry indifference
like nature's children – waiting
bolts of lightning love.

When endurance seemed at end,
swift surprise, like rain, came
with knowing speed; eager lipped
torrents of expression turned
the dark coat of questions
and by fulminant gesture
revealed its Joseph form,
radiant cascade of grace.

1999

MORTALITY

"and sudden friendships
measuring the first pour"

S. Creaves '99

94#   DREAMING DEAD

Today I sing
a chorus of dawns
to the dreaming dead.
Visions of mortality rise
smooth as a borning child,
yet the dead still dream.
The pain of eternity
like a sudden star
rests on their heart.

1971.

95#   FLOWERS (*to Harold Bartram*)

Flowers red and yellow,
twin colours of blood and soul.
Sorrow cuts clean
like the edge of a leaf
and every life hangs as if
on the point of a knife.

1972.

96#   JACARANDA (*to Cletus Henriques*)

Is death as delicate
as flowers we talked about
Wednesday last
— Water hyacinth
— Brazil Jacaranda.
How well I remember
your last painting
crafted with a knife.

And while bright rage
seeks to deny death,
the collective grief,
the corruption of flowers
do not concern those brethren
of particular soil
shouting in the wind,
whose shining trowels
replace the artist's knife.

1976.

97#   SHARPVILLE

Behind grim smoke,
soldiers with holes for eyes
sing the song of bullets.

Oh! the finality of the dead
whose knees no longer
point to the sky.

1977.

98#   WIND

Wind never is enemy
to waiting leaves
until fruit falls
in that awful hour.

Candleflies,
and shadows
howling like dogs.
Claws teeth and release.

1980.

99#   LOSS (*to Basil Hinds*)

Farewell flower of spirit,
fate decrees the flight of
the black orchid,
and another page is written
in the tortuous symmetry
of conditional peace.

I have grown a year tonight
listening to the seabirds
and cries of the woman-child
while, in some secret fastness
the muse sits smiling.

1981.

100#   IT

Like a ball bounced
by a friendly boy
is what it is.
A tumbled patch of earth
beneath watchful trees,
and words in the wind
fading to an evening sun.

1987.

101#   MAKER OF GUITARS (*to Louis Laroche*)

Chitara, guitara,
in the corner, sharing space
with my father's spirit
and his brother's before him,
dedicated protagonists
of this dread instrument –
both woman and coffin.

Chitara, guitara,
of symmetry in ancient woods,
framing songs of exaltation
as yet we daringly live
in bold fretted alliance;
This instrument fused to
each nerve and tapping foot,
all trapped in muted angles

or strange edges of this enigma.
Chitara, guitara,
daring all with its silence.

1987.

102#   BRIEF SPARK

From this brief spark
must I learn significance,
motivated by a force
in response to heaviness
not related to daily breath.
Are we born to joy,
or, seeing pain
recognise no change?
Yet, we know change
whose fantastic forms
dance like a miracle
we cannot reach
yet reaches us.
And a certain thing is done
that was to be done.
It is over.

1988.

103#   BUDDHA

Is it a fear of the one,
or a reading of no meaning
in the other.
Let us pray acceptance
and ride the roundabout.

1988.

104#   KNOWLEDGE PALM

In a life as sentinel, and
host to mute parasites,
in a youth of verdant fantasies
I fondled winds of the world
and called the sea, neighbour.
Final lesson of leaf and root
resides in eternal advocacy
of the silent seed
creating spreading passion
between light and earth.
I do not flinch from fatal shouts,
from steady hands,
waiting rope and axe.

1989.

105#   OFF-CAMPUS   (*to Bill Carr*)

Two-hand speed,
drinks and old doors.
Rum is a collection of used shoes,
journeys outside time,
and sudden friendships
measuring the first pour.

How much? With whom?
Tortuous bed of ethics,
ice, exuberant spit, and
dilemmas diagnosed from nine.

It is a real university between benches.
The other place is an obstacle to wind.

1990.

106#   ETERNITY

Rainbow atoms, or
floating world of fish-fins?
Who knows what it will be,
or when or where.

Thirty three seconds
inevitably invokes
that feral iron ball.
How many seconds
to eternity?

1996.

THE HARD YEARS

"The riddle is the tube
God's wheelbarrow
on a library roof"

S. GREER 97

107#   SILENT TIMES

Eyes opaque like scales,
the silent times are here.
Only stars speak,
and the living dead
now dead, cease to play.

These are the silent times,
when even songs cannot reclaim
the steady consciousness
of wild pointed diamonds.

1976.

108#   ASH, BIRD AND FISH

Wings of a jewelled bird,
the harp of the morning
rains my skin, with
a needle's touch
of understanding,
washing senseless scales
of corrupted truths.
Clouds have a way
of laughing at secret lies,
like black ash falling
from the antic hand
of some passing god.

1979.

109#   HUNTER

Cockerel and sun,
transgression is an open door
where fire flails
unwary feathers of foul birds.
The hunter's prevarication
lies in stems of issues,
and lopsided logic
parodies Logos the word.

1980.

110#   RIDDLE FOR U.G.

In the shadow of
a worm's cast,
the riddle is the tube.
God's wheelbarrow
on a library roof
contemplates the sky
as defined by sun.
Life-in-death on campus
stands survival slim –
the servitude of
benign biscuits.

1980.

111#   RIDDLE FOR L.F.S.B.

Exploiting political conditions
the looting continues.
Roach wings, beetle legs
are in the siftings.
The phone rings
to confirm an obscenity,
– What's the score?
– Flour gone!
and the myth explodes again.
Did the laudable fly
misconstrue my question.

1980.

112#   JESTER

Burn the day
when brotherhood is lost
for a wish that withers.
Forest and plantations nod
like old villagers,
to the dance of a cryptic jester
in an upside-down mirror.
His anxiety on wing
helpless to read
the language of flowers
and significance of stone.

1980.

113#   BECOMING

In the fork of the subjunctive
becoming is a choice
of rationalised absolutes.
Feathers read the air,
the bird dances.
Arrogance surrogates humility
on the plane of life,
Nature's geometry
falls silent, speaking only to
the wisdom of gnostic eyes.

1980.

114#   BICYCLE FOR L.F.S.B.

Winner be-spoked
in the fury of winning.
The cycle-wheel
of spurious speculation
turns rice-bowls
into songs about maggots.

1980.

115#   FOOD

Damning index of indifference
is our failed place.
Only marabuntas make pots.
Our blind theory of food
precludes the fashioning of clay,
and while the furious blades of rice
is evidence of wind,
where is our excuse to live?
Between thumb and forefinger
the forward pendulum stops.

1981.

116#   WISH

Black night, attenuated star, and
the dissolution of cultured bricks,
men stand at corners
daring time to reveal
the author of next year's rain.

I have watched rivers at work,
seawaves and leaves, but
nowhere in the land
have I found a song of man
flying on the nerve of wishes.

1981

117#   PLAY

Lizard-like,
an idea becomes a fly.
The urgency of time
conditions abnormal reflexes
and a wing rotates.

How long have I known
that play is every where,
sporting in nature
and iron toys.

1981.

118#   MR. CAT.

Reluctant pendulum
fusillade of flowers,
the agony is mine
in the name of a promise
and the silence of the cross.

In the valley of rats –
more-or-less congregation
under the eyes of the cat,
survival expels visions.
Scissors, breath and time
become one resolution.
Human rights for
dolorous rats.

1982.

119# MATADOR

Stars in sky-time
is the suit of lights
I dare not wear
at the matador's game.
As sand is to receive blood,
consequences sanctify actions.

The matador comes
with a bird impaled on a straw,
contemplates the dance
of convinced beggars
and the fatal symphony of dynamite.
His interest always curious
as a sudden spider
in an infinite crack.

Law is now measured
on a scale of laughter
in the corrida of games
where the matador smiles.
The bull is a self-indulgent shadow.

1982.

120#   ROYAL FOOL

I am the royal observer
of ambiguities and paradoxes,
the daunting knots
of purple intricacies, verse
and the colours of the fool.

In some secret desert
on some political pavement,
my footprint will mark
navels and rocks as
critical domain of truth.

1984.

LAND OF GREEN

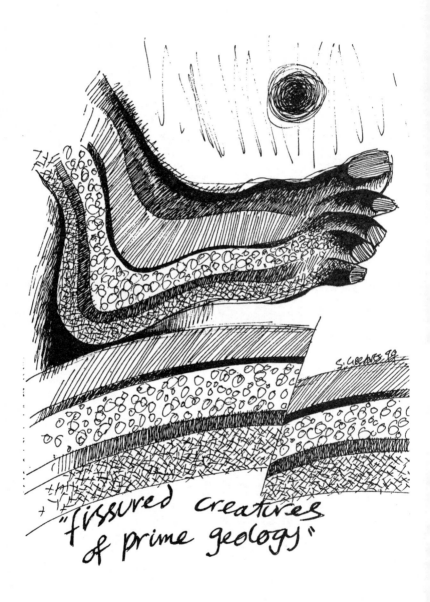

"fissured creatures
of prime geology"

121#   SOLDIER I

My bones will create symbols,
my blood-banner stains earth.
It is enough to know
the lifting of hands
will invite a song of bullets.

1967.

122#   SOLDIER II

Green lips of ferns
perform a benediction
in the fastness of the forest.
Aimed shells in sermon
create a damning tracery
in flesh and leaves.
My eyes accept the challenge
where the myth exploded
staining the earth now.

1967.

123#   GUYANA MASQUERADE

I am the great masquerader.
On a road of cobbled hearts
my feet draw sparks,
and dance syncopates
both pulse and drum.
Within palisades of teeth
men mock the dance —
rites of passage —
and rain copper coins,
flung with the arrogance
of empty minds.

1972.

124#   COOKSHOP

In a Chinese cookshop
composing poems
somebody's mother
asked me today,

— Gimme a small piece
— fo' some wine.

Sorry, no change.

— Gimme something
— fo' lil' wine nuh!

Sorry, no change.
In a Chinese cookshop

dreaming poems
somebody's mother
asked me...

1973.

125# RIVER SANDS

On flecked river sands
burdened with gold,
men dream and give
reality new clothes, but
old gods always rise
to demand ancient dues.

1973

126# MADMEN

Independence – May '66.
Republic – February '70,
yet certified madmen in '73
in a surge of personal identity,
wearing jackets worn and torn
roam the land in an air
of colonial gentility.
Long live the King!
Long live the Queen!
May the Mother Country
Never sink beneath the waves.

115

These are virtual realities,
for madmen always mirror
the secret yearnings of society.

1973.

127#   FOOT

No shoe,
I have seen a foot
toenails and heel,
fissured creatures
of prime geology.

I have seen a foot
walking this land.
I have seen that foot.

1974.

128#   TO POLITICIANS

A vortex of language,
seductive words of power
corrupt the tongue.
But words must leap fresh
— luminous lukanani in a pool.

Words must hit the air
– cosmic vibrations
of the gallant bell-bird.
Words must secure visions.

1976.

129#   SOLDIER   III

Fragments of a dream
shatter the mirage of horizons.
Words, map and blood
weave a deadly fabric of
lost shouts and ciphered corpses.
Metaphysical landscapes
of boots and bones
haunt the bloodied ancestor
and his progeny of steel.
Bright remorseless bullets
become propaganda that
dreams in matrices of stone
and aftermath of flowers.

1978.

130#   PORK-KNOCKER

Three hearts and flowers,
joy of an ancient day
when my songs are in
the book God wrote.
Tread softly sacred jewels,
star, leaf, and spotted jaguar,
the shores of desperate rivers
contain the serpent – counterpoint,
where more is nothing more than less
in the nest of concupiscence.

1981.

131#   PATRIMONY

What will the hedges say
when patrimony becomes
dust across the counter.
Will the warm ocean
keep secrets of
countless souls far away
dreaming of Demerara?

As roots do
beneath the feet of sheep
karmic debts do not sleep.
As we chart the suffering
of our age now,
a child's ear weeps.

1981.

132#   DREAM OF DEMERARA

In my land,
no known ghosts walk.
Our assumed history
is but a strange wind
that leaves no mark
upon an indifferent sea.
Even monsters dwell elsewhere
in another safe place,
where victims know themselves.

1981.

133#   GEORGETOWN

Voices we dream of
in the rationing of days,
pointing in packs
like black dogs in the city,
Without theorems of horizon,
that burning ship; Place
of burgeoning smoke,
is mirage and burden.

At the cardinal axis of crisis
belief retreats.
In the face of the transistor
myth becomes fossil.

1983.

134# KAMARIA (*to Ivan "Farro" Forrester*)

The forest is a secret blanket,
but rivers know the way
past blue hypnotic fungus
sitting in the magic of
green twilight thoughts
that hide horizons forever.

Precious things create links
with moments of hope and delight,
standing like proud citizens
of that sleeping edge, between
faced rock and fulgent water.

In the detritus of dreams
and the wakeful will of forests
are silent green leaves
on black tongues of the dead
stating the futility of search.
But impatient rapids know
why the left eye is of agate
and right of demanding gold.

1987.

135#   BOURDA MARKET

Visions of bread
in the marketplace,
voices hard as stones
summon hearts and shoes.
Amen! Amen!

to complex cripples,
whose hearts and heels
cry out for love
in dispassionate spaces
on today's pavement
of the market-square.

1988.

136#   RICEPOT

Forever in that easy diet of rice
what does it matter if an empty bag
hangs on my shoulder.
A universe is not stars in the night
but every single bullet grain
counted in a shaking spoon.

1990.

137#   OMAI

— *Patria o Muerte!*
Words of the revolution.

In some other places,
merely an indulgent noise
like fruit falling on tin roofs.
Monkeys crossing rivers
are more political.

—Bocas! Bocas!
Only the mouth of a dragon
can consume the spume
of that haemorrhagic river.

—Patria o Muerte!
Were is the revolution?
Let the toe ask the shoe.

1996.

138#   KNEES

Oh ! the knee,
      wondrous bone
      of flex and stern stasis
      happy to serve conscious form,
      potential moral weight or astute pretender.

Look ! by that microphone
      flying flags as god-sent signals.
      Political knees accepting
      words dangerous to truth.

Someday such knees will bend
      inevitable as any hinge,
      when messages take form
      as burden of stern hope.

Streets will sound to marching knees
Parents will dream for their children

and all will be right, perhaps,
in that dream if not this,
where knees of a weary people
threaten petty politics.

1998.

POT O' RICE

"But rum-jumbies
dance with people."

139#   COLUMBUS

On the infallible breast of Isis
below the horizon of constructs,
self conscious creations
of that possessed sailor
mimic inscrutable atoms.

My brother of maps
arrogant in discovery
ignores that incarnate world
that life chart in the very palm
grasping the navigating wheel.

1979.

140#   ICE-CREAM

Sweet mysteries
and stretched senses,
bell and ear
tongue to cone
and I far off, waiting.
A hearse's false aura
of abundant joy,
selling ice-cream
to sounds of twisted tape.

On waiting's sacred day
children come anticipant,
like wings and hummingbirds
at the trysting cave of a flower.

Hot soup of anxiety is a hunger
squeezing juices from joints.
Ice-cream — a symbol of longing
as death is for the aged,
welcoming the ultimate unknowable.

1980.

141#   TO POTTERS   (*to Bill Grace*)

Magic geometry
in a wasteland of desire.
Will the craftsman falter
within a flurry of unknowing.
Clay was ever sweet
despite the graveyard
that is the potter's field,
form is always the refuge
of a spirit assailed.

1983.

142#   TO ART MUSIC AND POETRY

There was a cat of clouds
playing with the moon, shadows
of wall, shutter and stairway,
as my mind hummed with
fragments the guitar sang.
I could not sleep
nor was I awake
to what the dream saw,

to the people in my bed
tuning the strings of art.
On silent steps in a painting
bananas watched toys
men always dream of,
and played them.

1984.

143# DANCING MAN

Before the mast,
in the presence of stars
and memory of a sacred tree,
a man dances alone, far
from the unforgiving dust
of metric cities.

Within prescient embraces
of a caring wind
and expectations of grace,
may hope grow to a moon.

1986.

144# CONVERSATION

Guitarists, Doctor,
on that verandah —
black dog singing in sleep.
A visitor inhales the night

as glass of old rum;
behind is a painting
of forms specific, but
ambiguity challenges.

— and yet they meet ,my friend.

— It s your concern, not mine,
this business about paradoxes.

— yours too, dear Doctor
fixing things with logic,
or knives.

— Do musicians care?

Ask the dog now dancing,
his brother dark night,
any other dark night,
and the equivocal efforts
of several moths.

1989.

145# BLUE SQUARE (*to Wordsworth McAndrew*)

Plotted canvas,
so square so blue.
I fix marks, from
the storehouse of time.

The will to art is a strange folly.
In the bewilderment of it all
archaic dreams re-assert
ever-present covenants between
mankind and the game.

1989.

146#   CARIBBEAN HISTORY

A flower falls on a leaf,
the forest sleeps, and
waves are on holiday.

El Dorado sings of love
as Columbus listens
in a plastic boat.
Guacanagari flies to New York,
– Nobody needs the Sargasso.
Juliet watches soap operas,
and wonders where
real heroes are gone.
Magdalene stops by a store
named, "Apostles' Feet".
– What are winged sandals for?
Exploring city slums
in a purple limousine
Cleopatra examines
all painted doors.
Other VIPs visit
St. Elsewhere-in-the-Sun
for rum and water skis.

There is no oracle,
only fraudulent cinemas.
Elections come –
now and then,
like bowls of free soup.
Old Moses says.
– Democracy works!
Citizens of some lands
stare in one-eyed belief.

But rum-jumbies
dance with people, and
– who don't see don't care.

1995

147#   THE REVO'

Over wasted minds in bloody animus
are born prayers, flags and guns.
Blessed bombs and dark cries
create sudden flowers of dust
in landscape stark as hairless egg.

Any rag on stick is "The Peoples' Flag".
Shouted words, feet and street
echo humanity's recurring loss.
Snatch rock, shoes, and run,
Run! for the revolution.

1997.

148#   MONTSERRAT

There was no blue
in the sky,
only a curious yellow,
more of earth
than anything else.

Like politician's speech,
that venting of ash/gases
smothers living and lifeless,
located root and pin.
A landscape of hope
once filled with imaginings
is no more. Everywhere
ash becomes ubiquitous shroud.
No house, no footprint
no child's cry of delight,
no rustle, no buzz.
Time out.

1997.

149#   ROOM

The floor was painted
with pepper sauce,
walls covered with soup.
Doors were biscuits
all cracked and flaked
and windows were
sliced pumpkin loops.
The room was illumined
by bunches of mangoes
and bright banana fingers.

All the guests sat quiet
at tables of smoked meat,
with knobbed bones for legs.
The chairs were clean roots
of cassava and yams and
everything looked so neat.
But the worrying thing
in everyone's mind was
what were they going to eat.

1998.

150#   THE SNAIL

Kitchen doors tight,
windows breathless,
and yet the snail sits
on a bag of old bread.
It has no wings — I said
nor thoughts I know of
like notions of arrival
demands of protocol
and sudden ownership.
Of viewer and viewed
who knows anyway
what the snail said.

1998.

Afterword

WORDS TO REFUTE CULTURES THAT WEAR BOOTS... THE POETRY OF STANLEY GREAVES

Stewart Brown

Born in 1934 in Guyana, where he lived and worked for most of his life, Stanley Greaves is one of the most important and accomplished of contemporary Caribbean artists. He is particularly renowned for his work as a painter, having exhibited widely in the Caribbean, Europe and the USA, with work in many public and private collections. He has won many honours for his painting, most notably perhaps the Gold medal at the 1994 Santo Domingo Biennale of Painting. But as the distinguished British critic Bill Carr observed in an unpublished essay on Greaves' poetry written in 1987, Stanley Greaves 'is a polymathic artist – painter, sculptor, potter and musician – on classical guitar.' Carr – who taught for many years at the University of Guyana, where he was a colleague of Greaves – went on to say, 'I have known for a long time that he wrote poetry. Individual poems – but that's like an architect walking about with bricks in his pocket while he meditates the finished house.' That 'finished house' is the present collection, selected and constructed by Greaves from the individual poems he has written over a thirty year period.

So this writing of poetry – while it has not been the primary vehicle of Greaves' expression – is a serious and sustained activity, its particular craft learned and honed through those several decades, just as his skills as a painter have been. I go through this biographical preamble to a discussion of the poems because I want to say that these are a painter's poems, but I don't mean to imply by that observation that the poems are in some way secondary to or simply a by-product of his work in painting. Rather, I mean that the predominant mode of narrative is painterly, a vivid making of pictures-in-words that we might expect from any fine poet, but crucially Greaves *trusts* the pictures that he makes. Implicitly, too, he trusts his readers to make connections between the images and textures and colours of the poem, or if not they must accept the paradox, the mystery, the occasion of the poem as enough, for as poet he will not belabour his points or strive to make plain what is so nuanced that it can only be said 'as poem'. Take for example his teasing autobiography – or it could be a succinct history of the Caribbean people – 'Origins':

> The origins are obscure,
> and lineage doubtful.
> All I have to reckon by
> is the colour of my mother's skin
> and the colour of my father's eye.

That must always be the attitude of the kind of painter Greaves is, one who aspires to do more than merely illustrate or decorate, who knows that the finished image, abstract or surreal/metaphysical, is capable of being 'read' in various ways. Indeed Greaves has spoken of his painting as 'allegorical storytelling' and that formulation also seems to me an apt description of what he is doing with his poems. Take the opening piece of the collection, 'Poetry', written in 1978, which serves as a kind of statement of intent – reminiscent of Martin Carter's 'Proem' – which lets the reader know what kind of poet Greaves aspires to be,

> In the time of revised spells
> when the language of poetry
> is no more the tool of fools,
> granite flowers will bloom
> on the mountains, where

determined rivers flow
in furrows clawed by jaguars.

Although there are resonances and cross-references apparent if the reader is fortunate enough to know Greaves' work as a painter, the poems stand scrutiny – both individually and in this very consciously crafted collection – on their own merits, as poems in the wider discourse of Caribbean poetry, indeed of poetry-in-English. As Bill Carr judged it, Greaves 'is a poet who provokes the total mind and detains the senses in beautiful rest.'

As they are organised in this collection, along broadly thematic lines, the poems span the whole range of Greaves' concerns as poet and artist. The poems of love and family and childhood memory are intertwined with the political and philosophical poems, poems of grief and praise, of friendship and paradox, the one group informing the other, so that Greaves' fundamentally holistic vision emerges from the 'pot-o-rice' that is the sum of his life and work's experience. Although they are not arranged chronologically, the fact that the poems in the collection are dated by year of composition does allow us to read the collection another way and compare the poems written in the 70s and 80s with the more recent work. It is evident from the more recent poems that Greaves has been committed to that long 'apprenticeship to the word', that there has been a continuing development towards the lean, crafted formality and wry wit that characterises his best work. A poem like 'Knees', written in 1998 and included in the *Land of Green* section of the collection, can be taken as an example. Beginning as a seemingly lighthearted praise-song to the 'wondrous bone / of flex and stern stasis' it soon turns into a warning poem, punning on the many associations of the expression 'bending the knee.' Wary of the tyrant's familiar recourse to 'words dangerous to truth', the poem threatens any 'political knees' that might buckle under such pressure with the inevitable retribution of a 'weary people's…stern hope'. The wonderfully spare image of the knee's bending, 'inevitable as any hinge' enacts that process. This is a poem that seems to link very clearly with a sequence of paintings – 'There is a Meeting Here Tonight' – that Greaves was engaged on at around the same time, though the connection is more a matter of atmosphere and tone than of any direct illustrative link. The imagery of the political meeting, the mixture of wit and warning, the invocation of dream both as setting and agency: all cross over between the two modes of expression. Not that the poem needs the paintings to manufacture its visual pictures

> Streets will sound to marching knees
> Parents will dream for their children
> > And all will be right, perhaps,
> > In that dream if not this,
> > Where knees of a weary people
> Threaten petty politics.

That last stanza inevitably calls to mind the work of Guyana's greatest poet, Martin Carter, who was a long-time friend and comrade of Greaves and, as Greaves is quick to acknowledge, a major influence on his life as well on his work as poet. There are some stylistic echoes in terms of the ways Greaves crafts his poems – the angles he takes – and inevitably a similarity of focus on the problems facing Guyana, but what Greaves really takes from Carter's example is the notion of the necessary commitment of the poet to his vision and to his calling. The opening section of the collection is devoted to poems, written over the whole period the collection spans, that are dedicated to, inspired by or in some way responding to Carter's life and work. In 'To A Poet M.C.' he describes Carter as the:

.... warden of words,
stringing poems,
as the precipitous wren
its galaxy of songs

But Carter is not the only writer to bear on Greaves' style and vision. Indeed, like Carter, Greaves is a cosmopolitan and very widely read poet, as Bill Carr observed in his unpublished essay,

'When I read Greaves's poetry I am much struck by what I must describe as affinities of the working imagination and the working hand. I sense deeply in the poetry Baudelaire and Rimbaud, with artists Chagall and Cézanne possibly plodding heavily behind the scene. The affinities I have suggested – and there are more – do in fact comprise a tradition, an order of insight and value. ...When I discussed what I have just written with Greaves he showed no surprise. The two poets were major affinities and the artists peripherally so.'

That list of 'affinities' might also have been made in relation to another poet and (albeit 'part-time') painter of the Caribbean – Derek Walcott. Perhaps it was something about that generation – the two men are almost contemporaries, Walcott just a few years the senior – that they knew themselves but also looked to far horizons and felt able to claim those 'affinities' wherever they found them. Some of that perhaps resonates in the title Greaves has given to this collection. That said, though they are very different as poets – and I don't think Greaves would claim Walcott as an 'affinity' – they share certain ways of seeing and saying. There are poems in Greaves' *Metaphysics* section here that remind me of a certain strand in Walcott's poetry, and the evocations of childhood in the *Pebbles* section are as vivid as anything in Walcott's great autobiographical poem *Another Life*:

Images of time past are stored
in the back of a lonely mirror,
like leaves of a forbidden book.

Other aspects of Greaves' life and work leave their traces in his poems; he spent many years teaching at one level or another, and we can guess the kind of teacher he was from the implicit answer to the question embedded in his poem 'Teacher',

Is it the teacher's task
to dilute innocence
in cultures of explanation,
or, secretly wish that
in a somewhere time,
innocence as fantastic bird
will take flight
to refute cultures
that wear boots.

Hanging on to at least a memory of that 'fantastic bird' is part of what it has meant to be the kind of painter and poet Greaves has become. Simplicity and a certain kind of innocence is also apparent in the several love poems included in the collection. One of the earliest poems included here is 'Lily and the Leaf', a beautifully tender declaration of love. But even here there is the strange and unexpected image:

When the sun becomes
A glowing blue worm
Cocooned by clouds

Similarly the poems of personal grief and those that respond to the political despair of the Guyanese situation often surprise us by the turnings of the language. Bill Carr commented on the freshness and liveliness of Greaves' poetry even when it addresses such themes; he particularly admired the rhythmic energy of the poems,

> sharp (of the icebrook's temper) precise and always moving   ahead. It never loiters – the temptation of the bogus experimenter.

That quality is evident in a poem like 'To Politicians' which condemns the 'seductive words' and 'corrupt tongue' of a certain kind of political speech, but contrasts it with a use of language which might well be a description of Greaves' own practice as poet:

> ….. words must leap fresh
> – luminious lukanani in a pool.
> Words must hit the air
> – cosmic vibrations
> of the gallant bell-bird.
> Words must secure visions.

These are not always easy or comfortable poems for the reader, but no-one, I think, would disagree with Bill Carr's final judgment on the quality of Greaves' poetry:

> 'Rare in its translucency and shaped integrity, the unillusioned clarity of mind and art of hand, Greaves accords us both, and the achievement is so fresh. It is a seeing, a long watching, and then a most scrupulous doing.'

Centre of West African Studies,
University of Birmingham
June 2002